Grumpy Bear

Best Friend Bear

Secret Bear

This book belongs to:

Wish Bear

Love-a-lot Bear

D1172256

Published by Scholastic Inc.
90 Old Sherman Turnpike, Danbury, CT 06816.

SCHOLASTIC and associated logos are trademarks and/or registered trademarks of Scholastic Inc.

ISBN 0-439-84302-2

First Scholastic Printing, June 2006

Care Bears™
Friendship Club

Love-a-lot's Caring Cruise

by
Quinlan B. Lee

Illustrated by
Warner McGee
and
Douglas Day

SCHOLASTIC INC.
New York   Toronto   London   Auckland   Sydney
Mexico City   New Delhi   Hong Kong   Buenos Aires

Love-a-lot Bear was planning a cruise on the
Ship of Dreams for all of her friends.

"Everyone, bring something you love!" she told them.
"We'll set sail at sunset. The loveliest time of day."

7

The Care Bears were very excited about the cruise.

They spent the whole day getting ready for
their LOVE-ly adventure!

Secret Bear went to her treasure box
and got her **secret star buddies.**

Best Friend Bear and Bashful Heart Bear went to the flower field and picked bunches of **tulips**, their favorite flower.

Grumpy Bear found his special **umbrella** for the cruise.

Cheer Bear gathered a flock of colorful **butterflies.**

"They're so lovely!" she exclaimed.

When Funshine Bear came to see Share Bear, she was whipping up her best batch of rainbow bars. "Would you come on the cruise with me?" Funshine Bear asked. "You are something—I mean, someone—I love."

"Of course,"
said Share Bear.

17

Meanwhile, Love-a-lot Bear spent the
day getting the ship ready for the sunset cruise.

SUN

"I want everything to be just perfect,"
she said with a nod.

A few minutes before sunset,
the Care Bears were ready to sail.

"Let's go!" Love-a-lot Bear said.
"Love is in the air!"

"Wait—we can't set sail yet!" cried
Funshine Bear. "Bedtime Bear and Wish
Bear aren't here to share in the fun."

"Oh no!" Love-a-lot Bear replied. "The sun is setting and it's the loveliest time of the day. Our sunset cruise will be ruined."

"But, Love-a-lot Bear, you've always told me love is like sharing," said Share Bear. "It's not about what you want, but what you want to give."

Best Friend Bear added, "And you told
me love is like your best friend—always
patient and kind,"

"You're right,"
replied Love-a-lot Bear.

"Love isn't about what *I* want, and it is always patient and kind. We'll just have to wait for the others."

Cheer Bear gave her a hug. "Cheer up," she said. "Love never gives up, and neither will we. They'll be here. I just know it!"

As they waited, the sun sank lower in the sky, and Love-a-lot Bear sank lower in her seat.

"There is no way we can take a sunset cruise now," she said sadly.

Finally, Bedtime Bear and Wish Bear arrived.
"Sorry we're late," said Bedtime Bear.

"Yes," said Wish Bear. "I wish we could have
been here sooner. But the thing we love was hard
to round up."

"That's all right," Love-a-lot Bear said.

"I'm glad that you came. But I'm afraid it's too late for sunset and too dark for a cruise. Let's all just head back to Care-a-lot Castle."

"Don't say that, Love-a-lot Bear!" Wish Bear cried.
"You know love is like a wish. It always
finds a way."

"We're not giving up,"
said Bedtime Bear.

"Sunset cruises are lovely. But nighttime cruises are nice, too—especially because we brought the moon and the stars to light our way."

The Care Bears finally set sail on their cruise under a beautiful, sparkly night sky.

It turned out even better than Love-a-lot Bear had hoped. "You were right," she told Wish Bear.
"Love always finds a way," Wish Bear replied.

"Moonlight cruises are the LOVE-liest," Love-a-lot Bear added with a giggle.

Can you be patient and kind like Love-a-lot Bear?

Love-a-lot Bear told all of her friends to bring something or someone they loved on the Ship of Dreams.

💜 What or who would you have brought?

The Care Bears helped Love-a-lot remember that loving someone sometimes means you have to be patient.

 Is it easy to be patient and wait for someone?

 How can you show kindness to others?

Love-a-lot Bear wanted everything to be perfect for the cruise.

❤ Did she get what she wanted?

❤ Has something you planned ever turned out differently than you expected?

❤ Did that make you feel happy or sad?

Bashful Heart Bear

Cheer Bear

Share Bear

Bedtime Bear

Funshine Bear